Click, Clack, PEEP!

Click, Clack, Peep!

Doreen Cronin

Illustrated by **Betsy Lewin**

Atheneum Books for Young Readers
New York London Toronto Sydney New Delhi

A
atheneum

ATHENEUM BOOKS FOR YOUNG READERS · An imprint of Simon & Schuster Children's Publishing Division · 1230 Avenue of the Americas, New York, New York 10020 ·
Text copyright © 2015 by Doreen Cronin · Illustrations copyright © 2015 by Betsy Lewin · All rights reserved, including the right of reproduction in whole or in part in any
form. · ATHENEUM BOOKS FOR YOUNG READERS is a registered trademark of Simon & Schuster, Inc. · Atheneum logo is a trademark of Simon & Schuster, Inc. · For information
about special discounts for bulk purchases, please contact Simon & Schuster Special Sales at 1-866-506-1949 or business@simonandschuster.com. · The Simon & Schuster
Speakers Bureau can bring authors to your live event. For more information or to book an event, contact the Simon & Schuster Speakers Bureau at 1-866-248-3049 or visit
our website at www.simonspeakers.com. · Book design by Ann Bobco · The text for this book is set in Filosofia. · The illustrations for this book are rendered in watercolor. ·
Manufactured in China · 1214 SCP · First Edition · 10 9 8 7 6 5 4 3 2 1 · Library of Congress Cataloging-in-Publication Data · Cronin, Doreen. · Click, clack, peep! / Doreen
Cronin ; illustrated by Betsy Lewin. — First edition. · pages cm · Summary: All of the barnyard animals are excited about the arrival of a new duckling, until the noisy little one
refuses to go to sleep. · ISBN 978-1-4814-2411-0 · ISBN 978-1-4814-2412-7 (eBook) · [1. Domestic animals—Fiction. 2. Ducks—Fiction. 3. Animals—Infancy—Fiction.
4. Sleep—Fiction. 5. Humorous stories.] I. Lewin, Betsy, illustrator. II. Title. · PZ7.C88135Cjt 2015 · [E]—dc23   2014012772 · ISBN 978-1-4814-4495-8 (Scholastic edition)

For Betsy and Ted
—D. C.

For little Ellis,
the newest "peep" in the Lewin clan
—B. L.

Click, Clack, peep!

Farmer Brown stuck his head out the window.
The farm was too quiet.
Everyone was watching the egg.

Not a moo. Not an oink.
Not a click. Not a clack.

Not a baa.
Not a cluck.
Not a thing.

Then . . . a crack.

Inside the barn
everyone gathered closer.

moo?

crack

baa?

crack

Baby Duck!

Baby Duck laughed.
PEEP PEEP PEEP
And laughed again.

Baby Duck waddled.
PEEP PEEP PEEP
And waddled again.

Baby Duck played.
PEEP PEEP PEEP
And played again!

The animals yawned.

peep peep peep

And yawned again.

The chickens sang a lullaby.

But Baby Duck would not sleep.

peep
peep
peep

The cows lowered the shades.

But Baby Duck would not sleep.

peep peep peep

The sheep knitted a blanket.

But Baby Duck would not sleep.

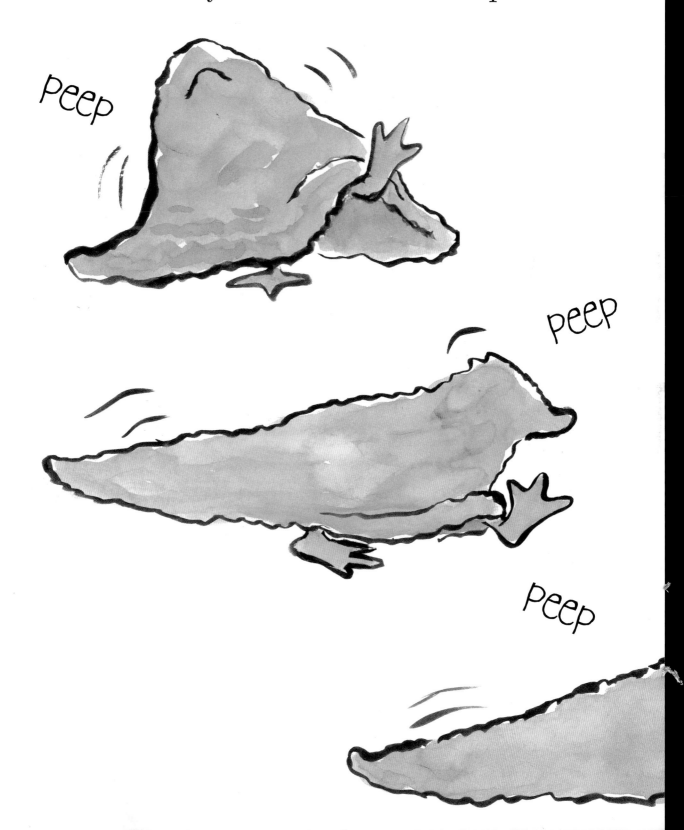

The chickens went outside to get some sleep.
The cows went outside to get some sleep.

The sheep went outside to get some sleep.
The mice went outside to get some sleep.

Duck took off his headphones.

peep
peep
peep

He put Baby Duck
into a bucket.

peep peep peep

He covered her
with a blanket.

peep peep peep

He carried her outside.

peep peep peep

He climbed
into
the tractor.

peep peep peep

He buckled up the seat belts.

peep peep peep

And backed out of the barnyard.

beep beep beep

He drove
back and forth.

peep
peep
peep

Back and forth.

peep peep peep

Back and forth.

peep, peep . . .

...*sleep*.

Farmer Brown opens his eyes
after a good night's sleep.

Not a moo.
Not a cluck.
Not a clack.

Not a peep.